LITTLE TREE

A Story for Children
With Serious Medical Problems

SECOND EDITION

To a very brave little girl, Carrie Inglesby

Published by
MAGINATION PRESS
An Educational Publishing Foundation Book
American Psychological Association
750 First Street, NE
Washington, DC 20002

For more information about our books, including a complete catalog, please write to us,
call 1-800-374-2721, or visit our website at www.maginationpress.com.

Art direction by Susan K. White.
The text type is Basilia.
Printed by Phoenix Color, Rockaway, New Jersey.

Library of Congress Cataloging-in-Publication Data

Mills, Joyce C., 1944-
Little tree : a story for children with serious medical problems / written by Joyce C. Mills ;
illustrated by Brian Sebern. — 2nd ed.
p. cm.
Summary: Although she is saddened that storm damage has caused her to lose some of her branches,
Little Tree draws strength and happiness from the knowledge that she still has a strong trunk,
deep roots, and a beautiful heart.
ISBN 1-59147-041-2 (hardcover : alk. paper) — ISBN 1-59147-042-0 (pbk. : alk. paper)
[1. Trees—Fiction. 2. Wounds and injuries—Fiction. 3. Self-esteem—Fiction.
4. Conduct of life—Fiction.] I. Sebern, Brian, ill. II. Title.
PZ7.M63977Li 2003
[E]—dc21   2003002216

Manufactured in the United States of America
10 9 8 7 6 5 4 3 2 1

LITTLE TREE

A Story for Children
With Serious Medical Problems

SECOND EDITION

written by Joyce C. Mills, Ph.D.
illustrated by Brian Sebern

MAGINATION PRESS • WASHINGTON, DC

ittle Tree lived happily on the edge of the forest. Every day her friend Amanda came to play with her. Little Tree sang songs to Amanda by rustling her leaves. And Amanda told Little Tree stories of adventures in faraway fields.

One day as Amanda and Little Tree were chatting, the sky filled with dark clouds. The wind began to blow very hard and fast. Amanda ran deep into the forest for safety.

Little Tree, being a tree, stayed where she was. All night long the strong winds blew and blew. Little Tree's branches were tossed from side to side, back and forth, and up and down.

The next morning,
the wind stopped blowing.
Amanda returned to
see how Little Tree had
survived the storm.

Little Tree looked different. Many of her
branches were broken and hanging down.
And many of her leaves had blown off. Amanda ran for help.

9

Two tree wizards
named Imageen and Fixumup came at her call.
Fixumup tapped on Little Tree's roots
and felt her bark. "Oooh," he said,
"your bark is verrry warm. But your roots are strong."

Next he climbed his ladder to check Little Tree's branches. He looked at them closely and moved them gently. Imageen put her ear to Little Tree's trunk. "Hmmm," she said, "you have a very good heart."

"We can give you herbs to cool your bark,"
said Fixumup. "But to really help you,
we will have to repair your broken branches
and take off the ones we cannot repair.
Then we will wrap them in soft leaves until
the ends are healed."

"I am afraid," said Little Tree.

"We can help you
with your fears,"
said Imageen.

"Amanda, you stay close to let Little Tree
know you are with her," said Imageen.
"Then, Little Tree, I want you to imagine
a picture in that cloud up there of what
feeling afraid looks like.
See its color
and shape."

14

Little Tree
concentrated hard.
Amanda stayed
close. Finally,
Little Tree said,
"I've got it."

15

When Little Tree
felt quieter inside,
Fixumup gave her
a special medicine
to help her feel sleepy
and comfortable.

Imageen told her to remember
to do her Magic Happy Breath.
And Amanda stayed close.

Then Fixumup
carefully removed
the broken branches
and wrapped the
ends with soft white
leaves, just as he
said he would.

During the next few days
and into the night,
Amanda told stories to Little Tree.
She talked to her when she was awake.
She even talked to her when she was asleep.
For, as everyone in the forest knows,
when you are asleep in the place
of dreaming, wonderful getting-better
things can happen.

Little Tree
grew stronger
every day.

But she was still sad. She missed her branches. Sometimes she felt as if they were still there. "Why were *my* branches broken?" she asked. "Did I do something wrong to make this happen?"

"You are a wonderful little tree, and it was not your fault," said Fixumup.

Imageen shook her head and said, "I don't know why, Little Tree. It is one of those questions that we do not know the answers to yet. What I do know is that you have strong roots and a brave heart. One day you will discover something very special about yourself."

Little Tree wondered what that special thing could be.

Some days later, Fixumup said, "Today is the day we take off the leaves. It is time for you to see yourself as you are now."

"You will see that you look different," said Imageen. "But it is an important and brave thing to do, to see yourself as you are."

24

When Little Tree looked in the pond, she did not recognize herself. She cried because all she saw were the missing branches. "Look deeper into the pond, Little Tree," whispered Imageen. Little Tree looked very deep into the pond. There she saw her strong trunk and deep healthy roots and her beautiful heart.

"Will my branches
ever grow back?"
asked Little Tree.

"No," said Imageen.

"But, Little Tree, do you see the branches you have left? Those branches are strong and can grow beautiful leaves and flowers. The flowers can turn into delicious fruits that you will be able to share with all of your friends in the forest."

Little Tree's leaves rustled happily when she pictured herself in the future. She wondered if that was what Imageen had meant when she said, "You will discover something very special about yourself."

After a timeless time, everyone in the forest
was happy to hear Little Tree laughing
and singing once again. Especially Amanda,
who was proud to have Little Tree
as her brave and special friend.

The Roots and the Power of Little Tree
by Joyce C. Mills, Ph.D.

Children who experience life-challenging illnesses or accidents can often feel overwhelmed and helpless. They particularly need help in dealing with their fears and confusions at such times. It is my hope that Little Tree's story will help children find comfort, inspiration, and an inner sense of well-being.

Originally inspired by a brave little girl of five who underwent multiple amputations, and by her compassionate and creative child psychiatrist, Dr. Geraldine Yarne, at Hartford Hospital in Connecticut, *Little Tree* will appeal to children facing many different challenges.

In this healing story, a little tree loses some of her branches in a storm. She experiences the emotions of fear, self-blame, and worry so common to children facing serious medical problems. Medical procedures such as examinations, surgeries, setting of bones, amputations, and skin grafting are subtly and symbolically mirrored, while messages of hope and healing are interwoven throughout the story. The tree wizards who help her represent the spiritual, psychological, and medical approaches to treatment so necessary in helping these children through their own journeys.

Little Tree learns that although she has lost many branches and leaves, she still has deep roots, a strong trunk, and a beautiful heart, and that she can still bear flowers and fruit. Children reading this story will discover that they still have their strengths, abilities, and resources for living fruitful and happy lives.

The Magic Happy Breath exercise, which the tree wizard teaches to Little Tree in the story, and which I describe on page 31 in more detail, is an additional tool that parents and professionals can use in helping children. It is an easy-to-learn relaxation technique that children can learn to help them feel comfortable, reduce their stress and pain, and draw on their inner strengths.

Parents may often feel their own fear and despair when their children have to face medical procedures or hospitalizations. As the parent of a son with cerebral palsy, I know these feelings well. Reading *Little Tree* to children and teaching them the Magic Happy Breath exercise are additional ways in which parents (and other caregivers) can participate in the child's treatment and healing process. It will also offer parents a sense of inner healing, comfort, and well-being.

Although *Little Tree* was written for children who are facing overwhelming life challenges, it can bring a message of hope to all who read it. It is my own hope that this story will touch your heart as deeply as the real-life tribulations of the brave little girl and her dedicated physician have touched and inspired mine.

Magic Happy Breath: A Relaxation Exercise for Children

To help your child learn to relax, you may say to him or her:

Get very, very comfortable.... Wiggle your body around until you find the best way for you (it helps to wiggle to demonstrate).... Good.... Now that you are comfortable, find something you enjoy looking at and let your eyes rest on that spot.... Now that you have that spot, begin by taking a Magic Happy Breath just like this (demonstrate): Breathe in through your nose and let the breath out through your mouth... just as if you were blowing a beautiful feather (hold your hand to your mouth as you demonstrate the breathing, pretending to have a feather in it).

Then you might ask:

What color is your feather? Does it have a sound? How does it feel in your hand?"

This helps give your child a rich sensory experience and distracts him or her from discomfort. After your child has breathed one Magic Happy Breath, ask him or her to repeat it three times. Follow the same basic instructions as before:

Find a spot to let your eyes rest on.... Breathe in through your nose and out through your mouth, as if you were blowing a feather in front of you.

Feel free to vary your suggestions to fit your style. Instead of a feather, for example, you might suggest holding a "fuzzy wish flower" and seeing all the "fuzzies fly away as you breathe out" or a "bubble wand" and seeing the "bubbles float off in the sky as you gently exhale." It is important that you breathe with your child while you do this exercise. This enhances the rapport between you and provides a visual model for your child in case he or she worries about not being able to do it or seems self-conscious.

After you and your child have completed this exercise, you might repeat it once again. This time, ask your child to close his or her eyes after the third Magic Happy Breath and:

Pretend to go on a magic ride to your favorite place.... I don't know where that favorite place will be for you...but I do know that you can go wherever you want...wherever you want to play and have fun.... Having fun seeing all the things you like to see...in front of you...in back of you...and all around you...smelling your very favorite smells...and maybe even being able to taste your very, very favorite food.... Take a few more minutes to play there and maybe even find a special something that you'd like to take back with you.... And when you are ready, take another Magic Happy Breath...as you open your eyes and return from your magic ride to right here.

This exercise can also be used as a lead-in to this and other stories:

Get as relaxed as you'd like to be...as you listen to the sounds inside as well as outside...and inside is a nice place to be...while I tell you a special story...a story about Little Tree....

The Magic Happy Breath is a wonderful way to give children a valuable tool for helping themselves reduce stress, worry, and pain while gaining a feeling of control in their young lives.

When Children Have Serious Medical Problems

by Jane Annunziata, Psy.D.

When children experience serious medical problems, they face a number of emotional challenges along with the physical difficulties of their illness or injury. These may include:

- Initial reactions of shock, denial, confusion, and disorientation.
- Feelings of loss of control (about being injured or ill, about this happening unexpectedly).
- Feelings of sadness and loss (loss of function; possibly literal loss, as in the loss of a limb; loss of life as it once was; loss of self-image; feeling damaged).
- Feelings of unfairness (Why did this happen to ME?)
- Feelings of anxiety and fear (about medical procedures, about death, that it could happen again, that the child will always look or feel bad).
- Feelings of anger (about the losses described above, the unfairness, having to endure so much, possible uncertainty about the future).
- Feelings of responsibility (Did I do something wrong to cause this? Is this punishment for something I did? Could I have prevented this, if only...?)

Parents grapple with their own feelings of shock, denial, anger, and sadness. Why did this happen to my child? Did I do something wrong? Could I have prevented this? What is going to happen to my child? In general, parents are comforted by seeing their own and their child's strengths, by seeing what is good and workable in their child's life, and by working through their feelings of sadness, loss, and anger—and helping their child to do the same—in the following ways. **Note: It is critical that parents get lots of support and nurturing for themselves so that they have the energy to nurture and buoy their children.**

Allow ample time for the child to grieve and mourn. Give him "permission" to have his feelings, and help him recognize and work through them by inviting him to talk openly.

Help the child harness her feelings of bravery and courage to face the physical and emotional trials, both now and in the future. Lend the child your strength when hers falters. For example: "I know you feel discouraged and tired right now, but I'm really hopeful that this new medicine will help" and "You'll feel better in the morning after some good sleep."

Maintain realistic optimism and hope for the present situation and the future. This will maximize the possibility of healing. Again, lend your hope and optimism to the child when his falters.

Help your child see her strengths, abilities, and unique gifts. Focus on what she still has and still can do. Help her see and embrace the positive in a real way: "I still can live life in these satisfying and meaningful ways" (help her articulate the specific ways). Separate her internal strengths and realities from the external medical problems and losses, just as Little Tree learns that her heart is still strong and that she can still bear fruit even with the loss of branches.

Provide tools and outlets to facilitate the child's emotional as well as physical healing, including imagery and relaxation exercises such as the Magic Happy Breath in this book, drawing and writing of feelings, storytelling, playing out of medical procedures, and professional help (if needed).

Help the child get outside of himself and the problem by focusing on doing something for others, such as drawing a picture or baking cookies for an elderly neighbor who is lonely. This can help mitigate his own feelings of sadness and loss. This does not apply to all situations, and it generally comes later in the healing process. Also, keep in mind that it can be difficult for kids to do. In the first place, children who are in their own pain or struggling with a medical problem may be in too much distress to reach out to others. Second, for this to be possible, the child must have been helped to acknowledge and work through all of the psychological issues described above.

Jane Annunziata, Psy.D., is a clinical psychologist with a private practice for children and families in McLean, Virginia. She is also the author of several books and articles addressing the concerns of children and parents.